No More Noisy Nights

Written by Holly L. Niner Illustrated by Guy Wolek

Flash
Light PRESS

For my friends, who make the days – and nights – better! –HLN

To my wife and best friend, Debi. I don't know where I'd be without you.
I love you so much, doll. –GW

Copyright © 2017 by Flashlight Press | Text copyright © 2017 by Holly L. Niner | Illustrations copyright © 2017 by Guy Wolek
All rights reserved, including the right of reproduction, in whole or in part, in any form. Printed in China. First Edition September 1, 2017
Editor: Shari Dash Greenspan | Graphic Design: The Virtual Paintbrush | Distributed by IPG · www.ipgbook.com
ISBNs: Hardcover 9781936261932, ePDF 9781936261949, EPUB 9781936261956, Mobipocket 9781936261963
Cataloging-in-Publication data is available from the Library of Congress.
The fonts are Fontesque and WinstonNero.
The illustrations were created digitally.
Flashlight Press · www.FlashlightPress.com
527 Empire Blvd., Brooklyn, NY 11225
Free printable activity pages available
on our website.

Jackson worked hard all day moving into his new house.

After dinner,
he relaxed.

And at nine o'clock, he climbed into bed.

That's when he heard...

OOOEEEeee OOOEEEeee OOOEEEeee OOOOOOOOOO

"Oh dear," Jackson said. "There must be a ghost in the attic. I hope this noise stops soon."

But it didn't.

So Jackson stuffed his ears with cotton balls and tried to sleep.

The next morning, Jackson was so tired he poured orange juice on his cereal and ketchup on his toast.

After breakfast, Jackson peeked into the attic. "Sorry to disturb you, Mr. Ghost, but could you please stop OOOEEEeee OOOEEEeee OOOing all night? I would like to sleep."

"OOOEEEeee. I'm sorry," said the ghost. "But what else can I do?"

"Let me think about that," said Jackson.

Jackson thought about it all day while he unpacked.

After dinner,
he put a box on
the attic floor.

Then he relaxed
in his favorite chair.

And at nine o'clock, Jackson climbed into bed. That's when he heard...

BOOGETY WOOGETY WOOOOOOOO

"Oh dear," Jackson said. "There must be a boogey monster in the basement. I hope this noise stops soon."

But it didn't.

So he stuffed his ears with cotton balls,
pulled on his thickest ski cap,
and tried to sleep.

The next morning, Jackson was so tired he could barely open his eyes to pick out his clothes.

After breakfast, Jackson tiptoed down the stairs.
"Sorry to disturb you, Mr. Monster, but could you please stop
BOOGETY WOOGETY WOOing all night? I need to sleep."

"BOOGETY WOOGETY WHOOPS,"
said the boogey monster. "But what else can I do?"

"Let me think about that," said Jackson.

Jackson thought about it all day while he unpacked.

ZZZZZZZZZZ

After dinner, he left a box at the bottom of the basement stairs.

Then he relaxed in his favorite chair.

And at nine o'clock, he climbed into bed. That's when he heard...

"Oh dear," said Jackson.
"There must be a pixie
in the piano. I hope this
noise stops soon."

But it didn't.

So he stuffed his ears with cotton balls, pulled on his thickest ski cap, wrapped his pillow around his head, and tried to sleep.

The next morning, Jackson was SO tired he washed his face with toothpaste and brushed his teeth with soap!

After breakfast, Jackson peeked into the piano. "Sorry to disturb you, Miss Pixie, but could you please stop PLINK PLUNKing all night? I really need to sleep."

"Plink plunk, pardon me,"
said the piano pixie.
"But what else can I do?"

"Let me think about that," said Jackson.

Jackson thought about it
all day while he unpacked.

After dinner, he put some sheet music on the piano.

But he was too tired to relax in his favorite chair, so Jackson climbed straight into bed.

That's when he just barely heard...

...the gentle thup of puzzle pieces,
the quiet chugga-chugga of a toy train,
and the soothing sounds of
a pixie lullaby.

Jackson sighed. He closed his eyes.
And he finally fell asleep in his new
house with his not-so-noisy...